What Shall We Do, Blue Kangaroo?

EMMA CHICHESTER CLARK

for Mr and Mrs Brown,
Lily and Jack

Have you read these picture books by Emma Chichester Clark?

More!

Follow My Leader!

No More Kissing!

I Love You, Blue Kangaroo!

Where Are You, Blue Kangaroo?

It Was You, Blue Kangaroo!

First published in hardback in Great Britain by Andersen Press Ltd in 2002
First published in paperback by Collins Picture Books in 2004

3 5 7 9 10 8 6 4
ISBN: 0-00-716194-8

Collins Picture Books is an imprint of the Children's Division, part of HarperCollins Publishers Ltd.
Text and illustrations copyright © Emma Chichester Clark 2002
The author/illustrator asserts the moral right to be identified as the author/illustrator of the work
A CIP catalogue record for this title is available from the British Library.
Visit our website at: www.harpercollinschildrensbooks.co.uk
Printed and bound in Hong Kong

Blue Kangaroo belonged to Lily.
He was her very own kangaroo.
Sometimes, when Lily didn't know what to do next,
she would say, "What shall we do, Blue Kangaroo?"
But Blue Kangaroo didn't know, so he said nothing.

Lily went to see what Aunt Florence was doing.
"Will you draw a dinosaur for me?" asked Lily.

"Not just now," said Aunt Florence. "Maybe later."
"Oh well," said Lily, "I'll have to try and do it by myself."

Lily drew five dinosaurs, all by herself . . .

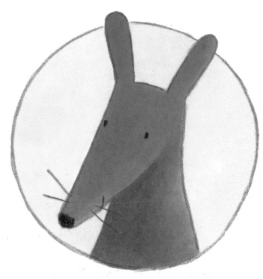

. . . and Blue Kangaroo
thought, "How clever she is!"

"That's enough of drawing," said Lily.
"Now what shall we do, Blue Kangaroo?"
But Blue Kangaroo didn't know, so he said nothing.

Lily went to see what Aunt Jemima was doing.
"Can you help me make a picnic?" asked Lily.

"I'm a bit busy just now," said Aunt Jemima.
"Oh," said Lily. "Then I'll just have to do it by myself."

Lily arranged all the animals and gave them their tea,
all by herself . . .

. . . and Blue Kangaroo thought,
"She did *that* very well!"

When the animals had finished eating and everyone was full, Lily said, "Now what shall we do, Blue Kangaroo?" But Blue Kangaroo didn't know, so he said nothing.

Lily went to see what her mother was doing.
She was helping Uncle George.
"Will you read my book to me?" asked Lily.

"Not at the moment, Lily," said her mother.
"But I bet you can read that book all by yourself."

Lily wasn't sure but she began to read.
She discovered she *could* do it.

"All by herself!"
thought Blue Kangaroo.
He loved being read to.

Suddenly, Lily noticed that it was raining outside.
"Someone help me get the animals in!" she cried.

But nobody came.

"I'll just have to do it myself," said Lily.

She put all the wet animals into her wheelbarrow . . .

. . . and ran back into the house.

Then she lined them up on the warm radiator to dry . . .

. . . and Blue Kangaroo
noticed that someone
was missing.

"Now what shall we do, Blue Kangaroo?" asked Lily.
"I wonder what Daddy is doing . . ."

Her father was trying to get the baby to stop crying.
"Oh, Lily!" he said. "What shall we do?"

"I'll read to him," said Lily.

"Can you read all by yourself?" asked her father.

"Yes," said Lily. "All by myself!"

Soon Lily's little brother was fast asleep.
"Thank you, Lily," said her father. "You *are* clever.
I don't know what I'd do without you."

When Lily's mother tucked her up in bed that night she said, "Thank you for being so good today . . ."

. . . and Blue Kangaroo thought, "She's forgotten Tiny Teddy. What shall we do?"

But Lily had fallen asleep, so she said nothing.
When the house was quiet, Blue Kangaroo
hopped out of bed.

"I'll just have to rescue him all by myself," he thought.

It was dark and still raining,
but Blue Kangaroo found Tiny Teddy.
He dragged him across the garden
and pulled him through the cat-flap.
Then he propped him up against
the radiator to dry.

When Lily woke up the next morning, she found a wet kangaroo beside her.
"What have you been doing, Blue Kangaroo?" she asked.

It was only when she went downstairs that she realised what had happened. "Oh, poor Tiny Teddy!" said Lily.

Lily kissed Blue Kangaroo's damp nose.
"You are *clever*, Blue Kangaroo!" said Lily.
"What would I do without you?"
Blue Kangaroo didn't know, so he said nothing.